RWELL

This edition published by Parragon Books Ltd in 2015

Parragon Books Ltd
Chartist House
15–17 Trim Street
Bath BA1 1HA, UK
www.parragon.com

ISBN 978-1-4748-1853-7

Printed in China

# MARVEL

# STORYBOOK COLLECTION

Parragon

Bath • New York • Cologne • Melbourne • Delhi
Hong Kong • Shenzhen • Singapore • Amsterdam

# CONTENTS

# IRON MAN

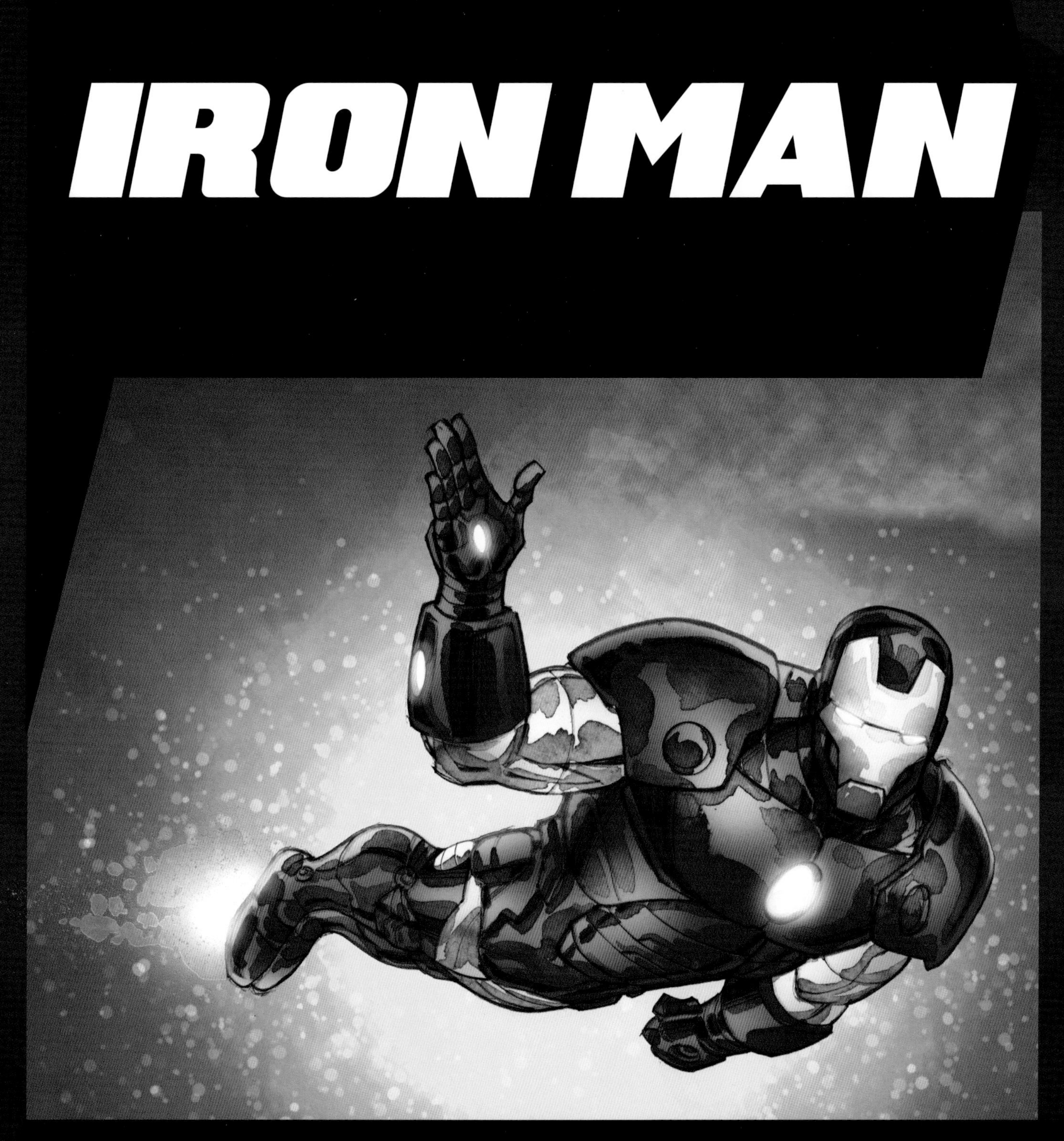

## ORIGIN STORY

This is Tony Stark. Tony is usually a regular guy – only with a lot more money.

But when Tony puts on his special armour, he becomes more powerful than most other people. He even has a different name. When Tony puts on his armour, he becomes ...

## ... the Invincible Iron Man!

Tony wasn't born a super hero. He hasn't always fought to protect people. But with villains on the loose, like Titanium Man and Iron Monger – who use Tony's technology for their own, evil purposes – Tony feels it is his responsibility to stop them.

Tony didn't always get the job done this easily. Or this well. Tony's armour wasn't always so sleek. In fact, when he first became Iron Man, Tony's armour didn't even shine!

But if you really want to know how Iron Man was born, we need to start with the man behind the mask. We need to start with Tony.

Tony had so much money that he could go anywhere he wanted.

He loved to have fun. And he loved the finer things in life.

But Tony also worked hard. He was a brilliant inventor and he knew all sorts of things about science.

He loved to work with magnetic fields. Using them, he created a powerful energy force that he called 'repulsor technology'.

The military was interested in Tony's work. In fact, it was in a secret army lab that Tony's life was changed forever. An enemy army attacked and Tony was badly hurt!

Since Tony was famous, he was recognized right away. The enemy knew all about his inventions. They tossed him in a prison cell filled with electronic and mechanical equipment. They wanted him to create a mighty weapon for them.

To make things worse, they told Tony that his heart had been hurt in the blast. He didn't have much longer to live.

Tony soon found he was not alone in the cell. The enemy had captured another famous scientist – Professor Yinsen. The enemy wanted the two men to work together on the great weapon.

But Professor Yinsen had other ideas – he knew a way to keep Tony alive!

The two men worked tirelessly to create something that would save Tony's life and, at the same time, help them to escape the prison.

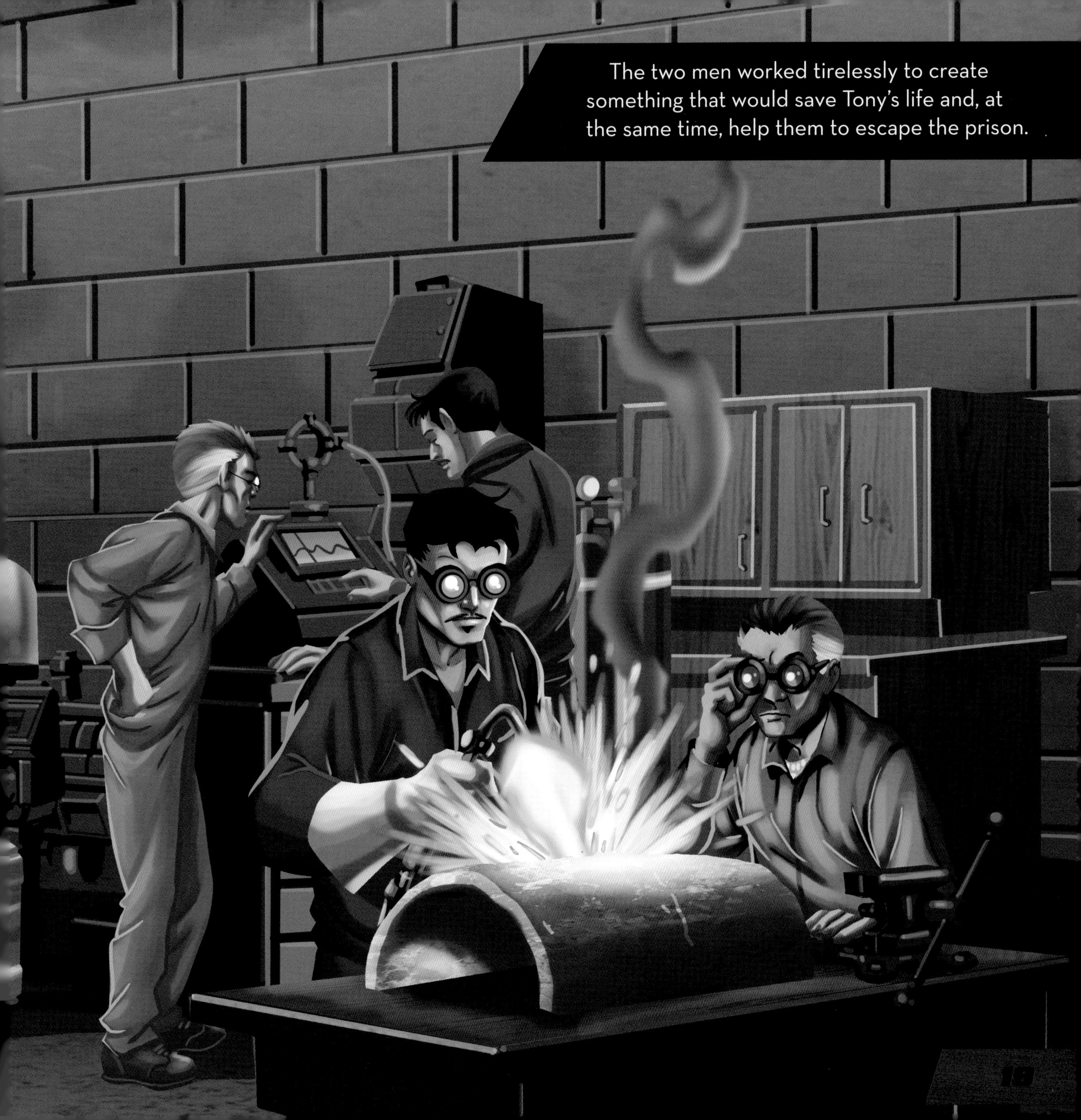

Finally, the men completed the device that Tony would always need to wear on his chest in order to keep his heart beating. But that wasn't all they had created.

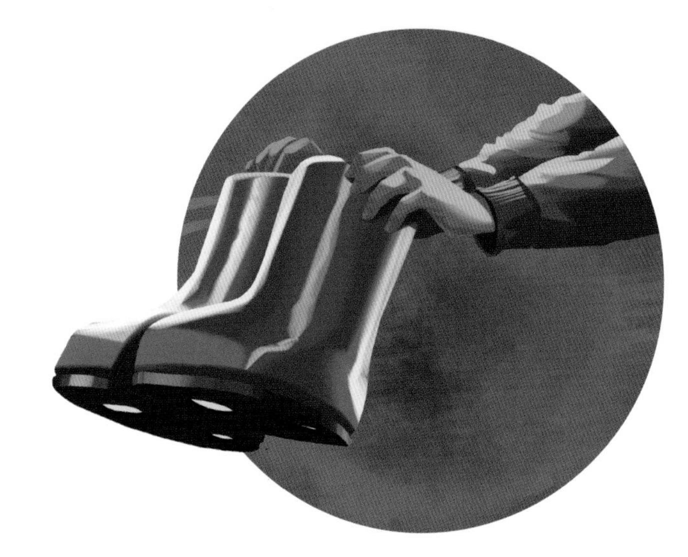

Using Tony's repulsor technology, they had built boots that could help a man fly!

Gloves that could crush steel!

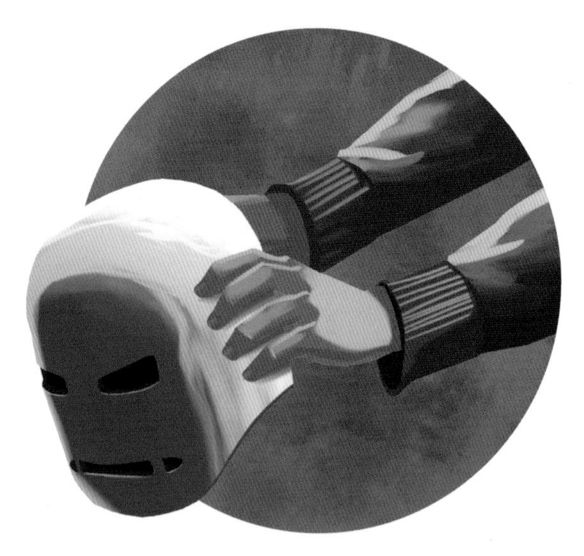

And a helmet that could protect a man from the most terrible blast!

Tony put on the armour and proved that no walls could hold ...

… the Iron Man! It wasn't long before the enemy realized they were fighting a losing battle.

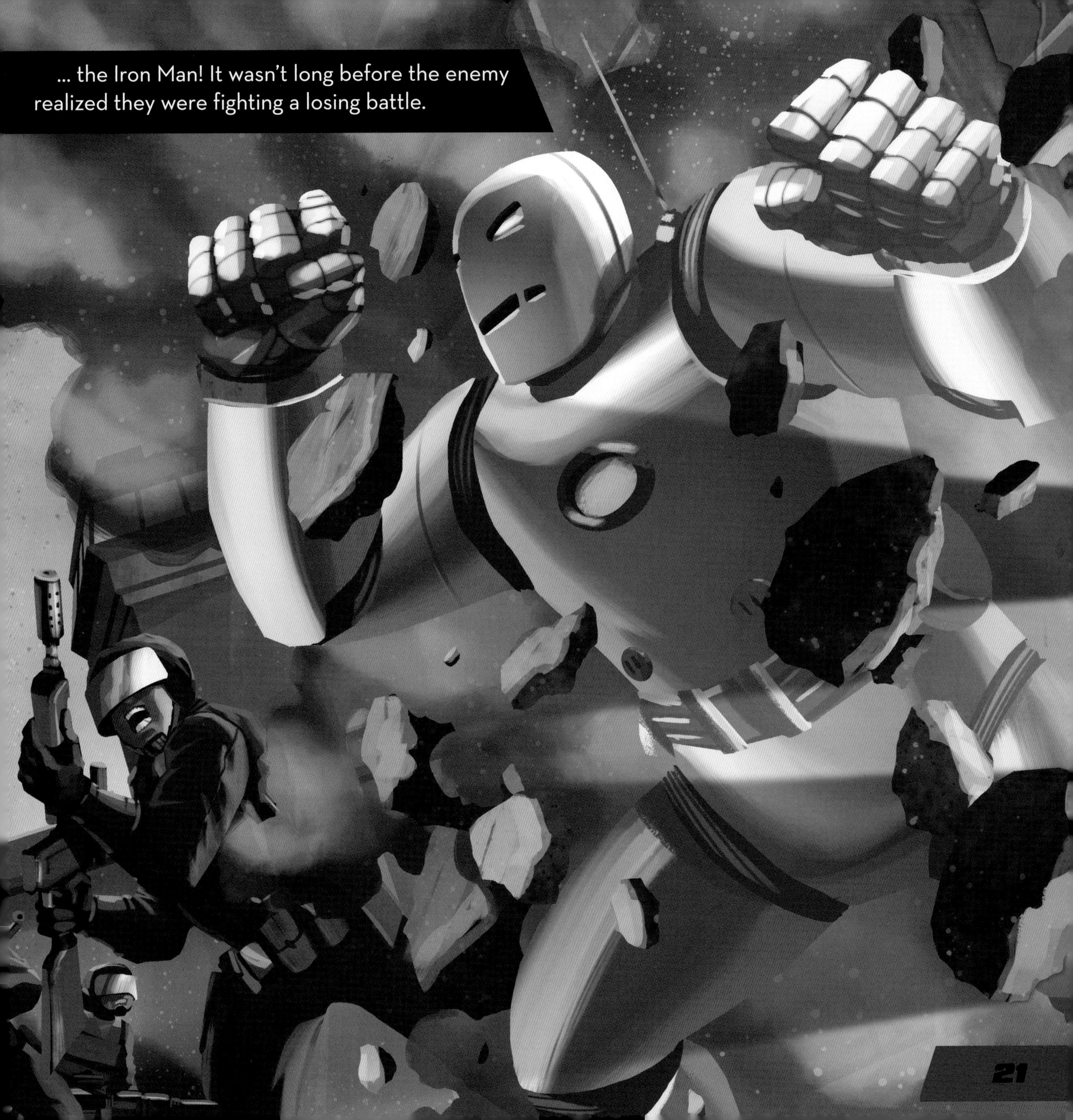

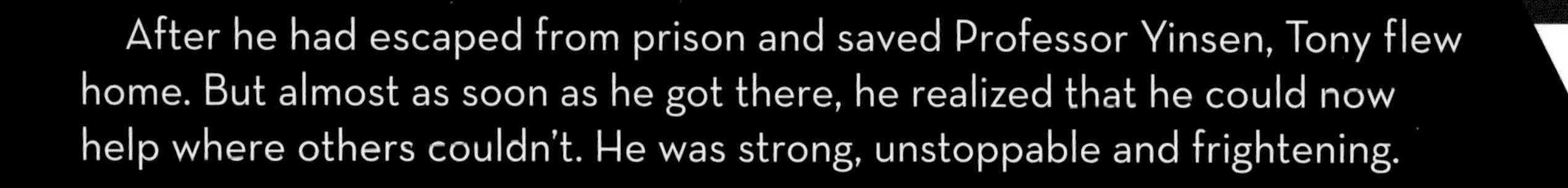

After he had escaped from prison and saved Professor Yinsen, Tony flew home. But almost as soon as he got there, he realized that he could now help where others couldn't. He was strong, unstoppable and frightening.

But maybe he was a little too frightening. Tony didn't want innocent people to be scared of him. He decided the suit needed to change.

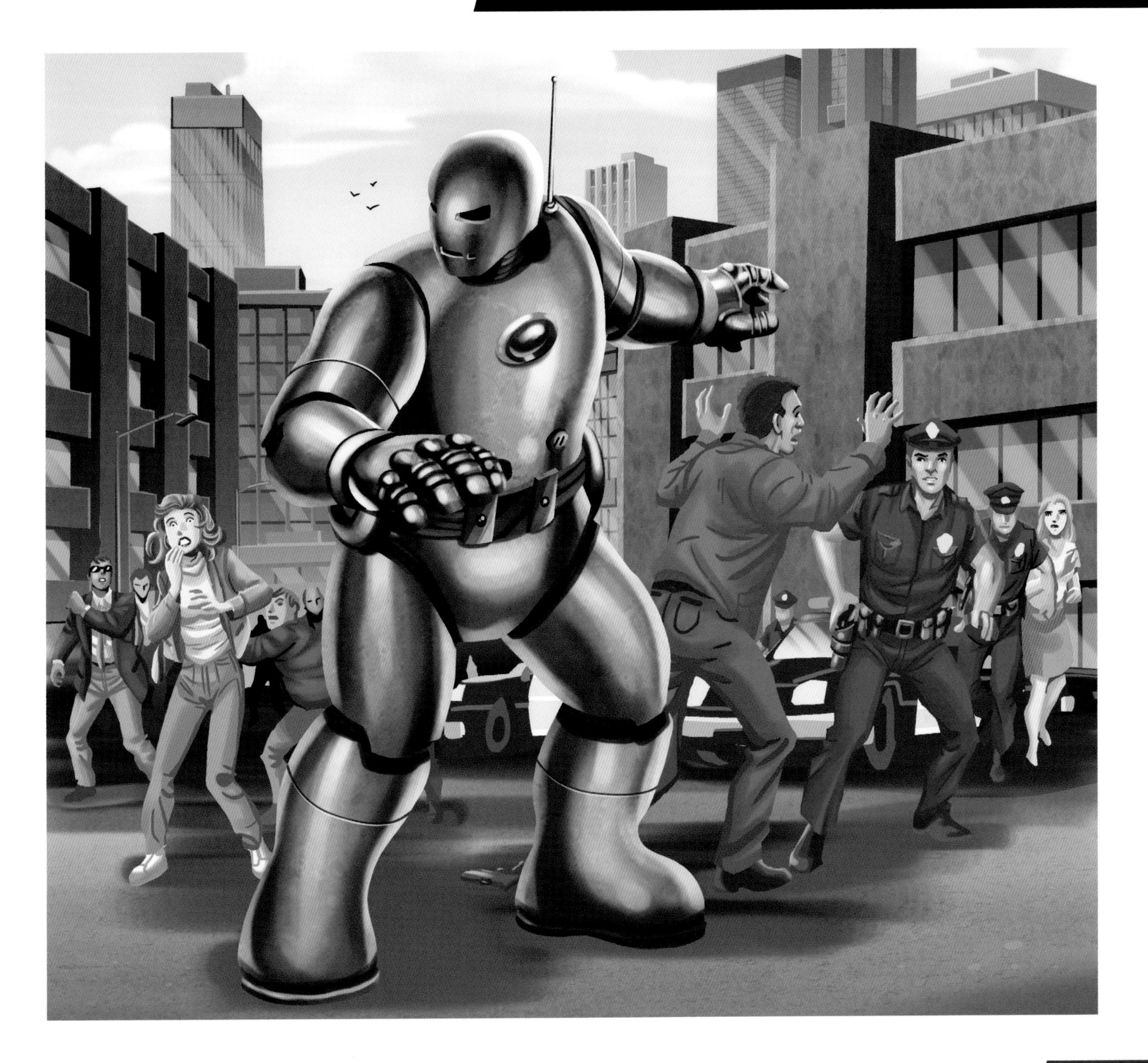

Tony thought that Iron Man needed something as smooth and stylish as he was. He needed to create a lighter suit.

Although his chest plate couldn't change, everything around it could.

Soon, Tony perfected the armour ...

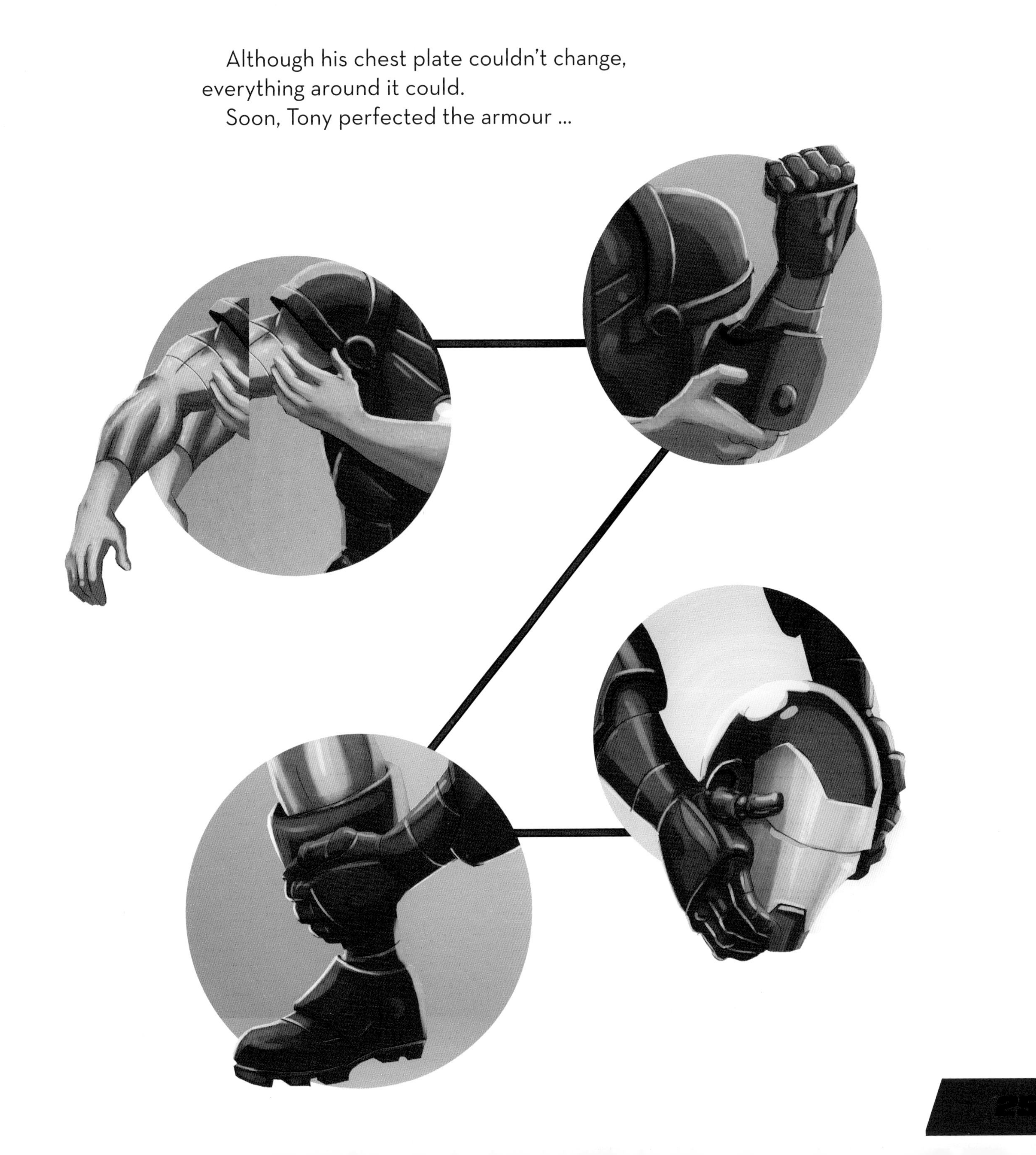

... and the Invincible Iron Man was born again!

And as Iron Man, Tony never stops fighting. He protects people at home and around the world.

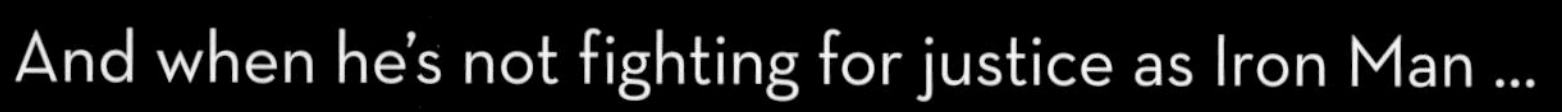

And when he's not fighting for justice as Iron Man ...

... Tony runs his company, Stark Industries.

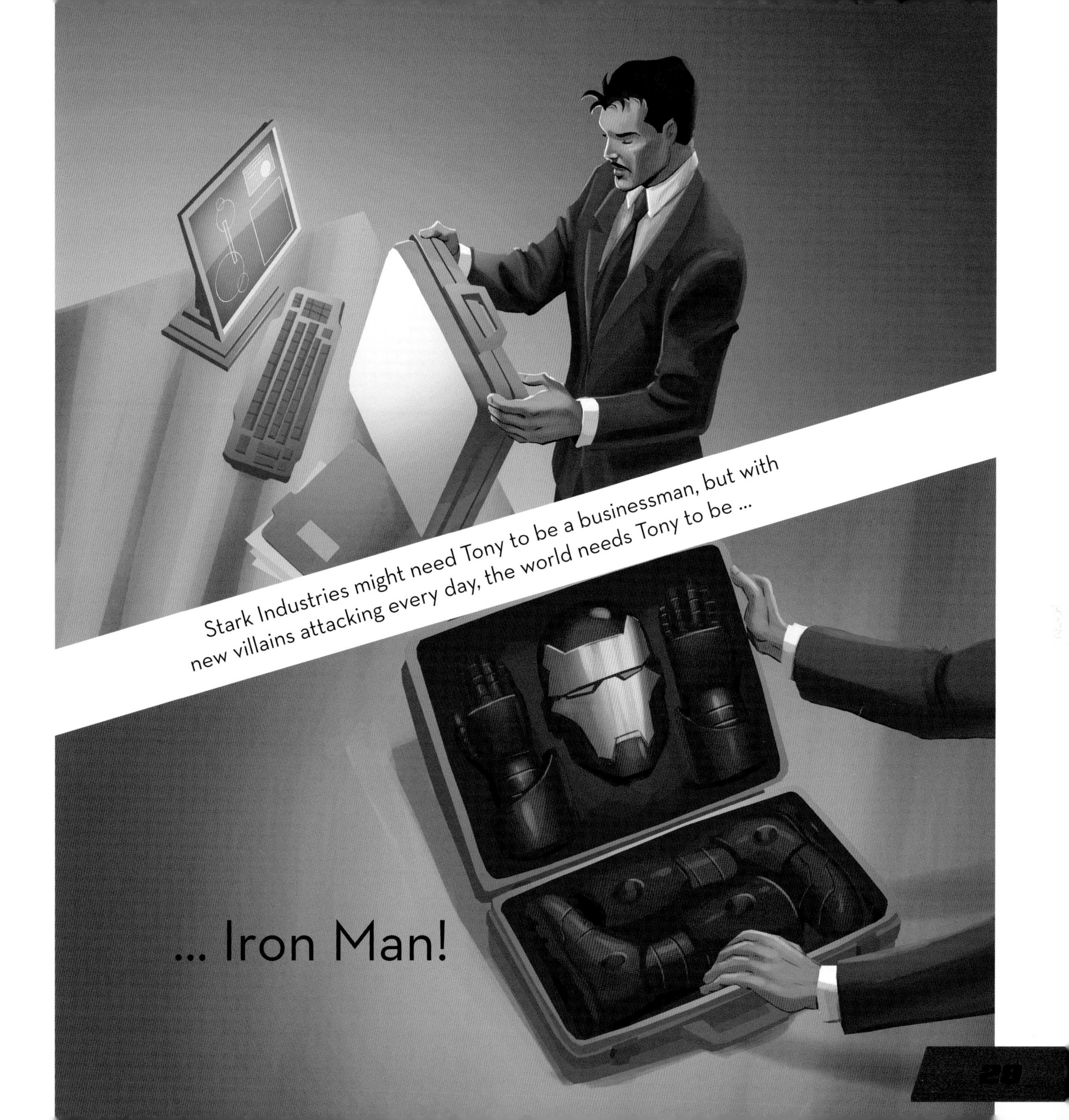
Stark Industries might need Tony to be a businessman, but with new villains attacking every day, the world needs Tony to be ...
... Iron Man!

# CAPTAIN AMERICA

## ORIGIN STORY

Before you were born – in fact, long before even the oldest person you know had been born – a peaceful little island sat just off the mainland of a place that was called different things by all the different people who lived there.

As time went on, more and more people came to this little island.

They wanted to leave behind the lives they led in a place they called the Old World and build new ones in a place where they believed anything was possible.

They came from all over the world. For most, this island was the first stop on the path to a new life in this young nation.

This island was known as Manhattan, in the city of New York. The country would be known as the United States of America – or America, for short.

Before America was even two hundred years old, it was called upon to fight alongside other countries in a terrible war that was destroying the world.

The news of war moved people. It seemed like everyone in the country wanted to join the army to help.

Including a young man named Steve Rogers.

Steve had been upset about the war for some time. Now that America was involved, he could do something about it.

Soon, Steve was in a long queue of men waiting to be examined. If the men passed, they would be deployed to the war.

Steve waited his turn.

Every man so far had passed.

Steve was confident he would, too.

But after examining Steve, the doctor told him that he was in no shape to join the army.

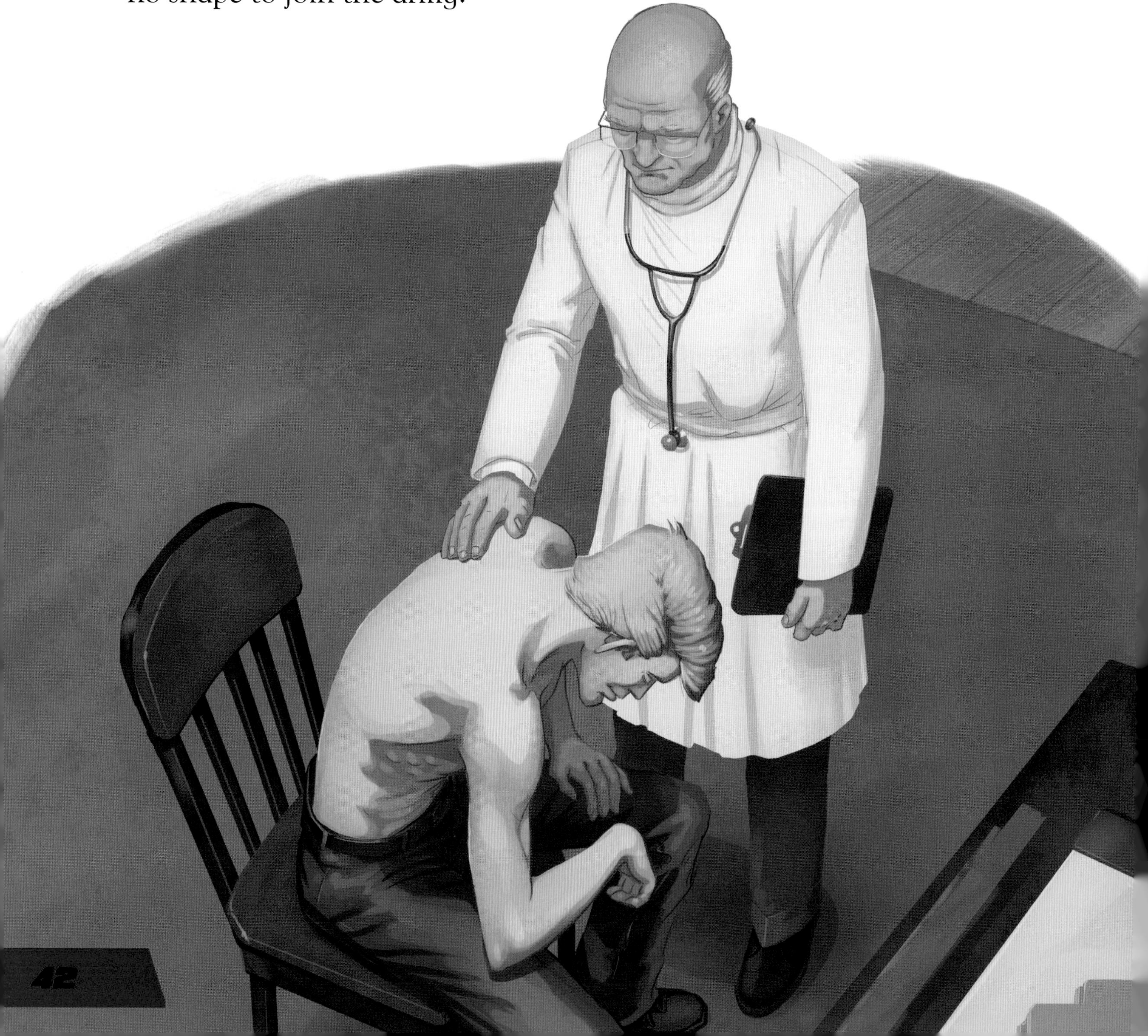

But then he told him there was another way to get into the army. He handed Steve a file marked

**CLASSIFIED – PROJECT: REBIRTH.**

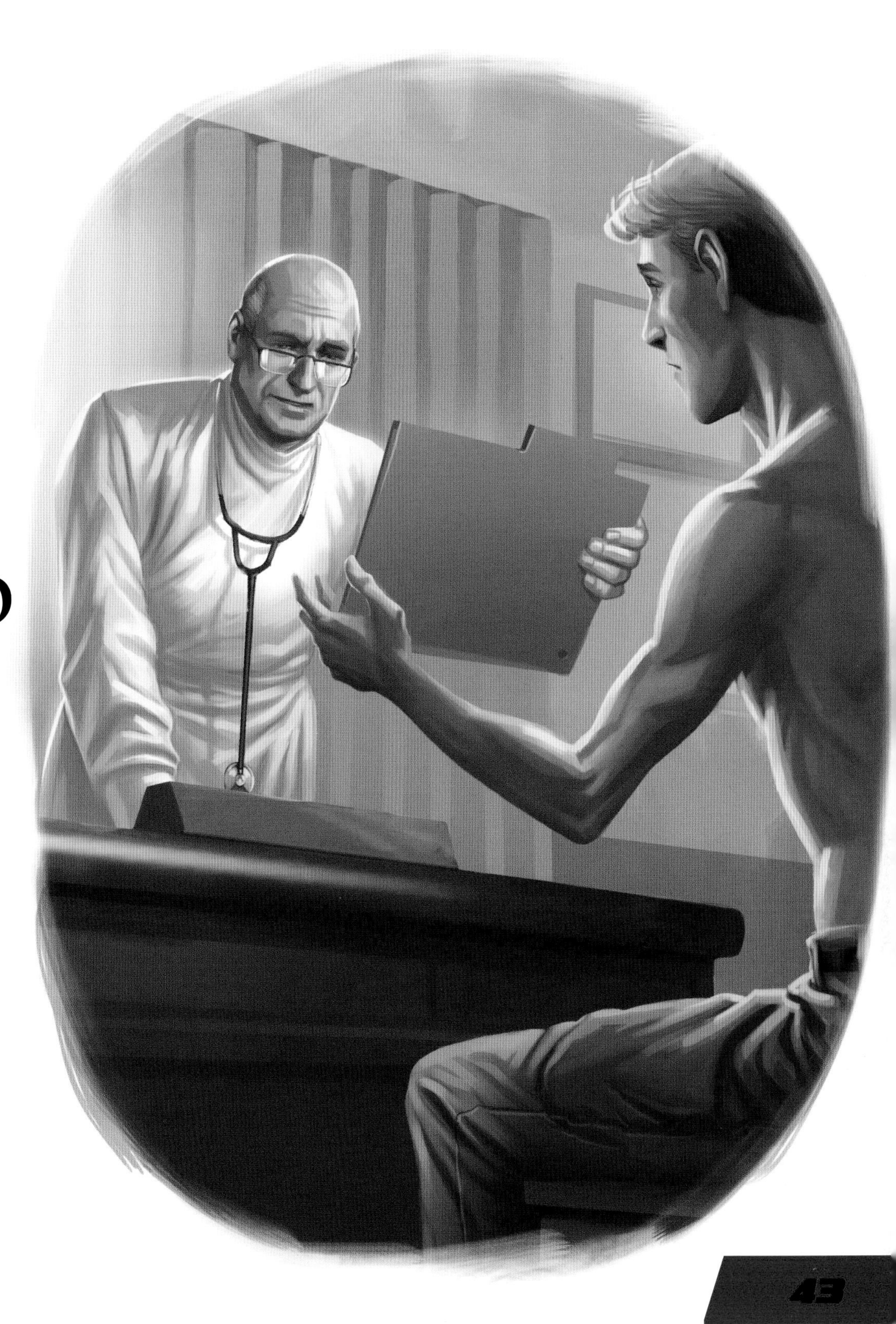

The doctor told Steve that if the experiment worked, he would be able to join the army.

Steve said he would try anything to become a soldier. The doctor called in a general named Chester Phillips. General Phillips was in charge of Project: Rebirth.

The general led Steve down a hidden hallway to a secret exit.

Soon the two men were crossing the bridge into nearby Brooklyn.

They arrived at an antiques shop in a run-down, dangerous-looking area. An old woman let them in and led them downstairs.

But the shopfront was not an antiques shop at all! It was a cover for an underground lab.

And the owner was not an old woman, but a secret agent!

General Phillips introduced Steve to the project's lead scientist, Doctor Erskine.

He told Steve that the Super-Soldier serum, combined with the Vita-Rays ...

... would transform him from frail

and sickly ...

... into America's

The experiment was a SUCCESS!

But before Steve, General Phillips or anyone else in the lab could notice, an enemy spy who had been working in the lab attacked!

The doctor was hurt and unable to duplicate the serum.

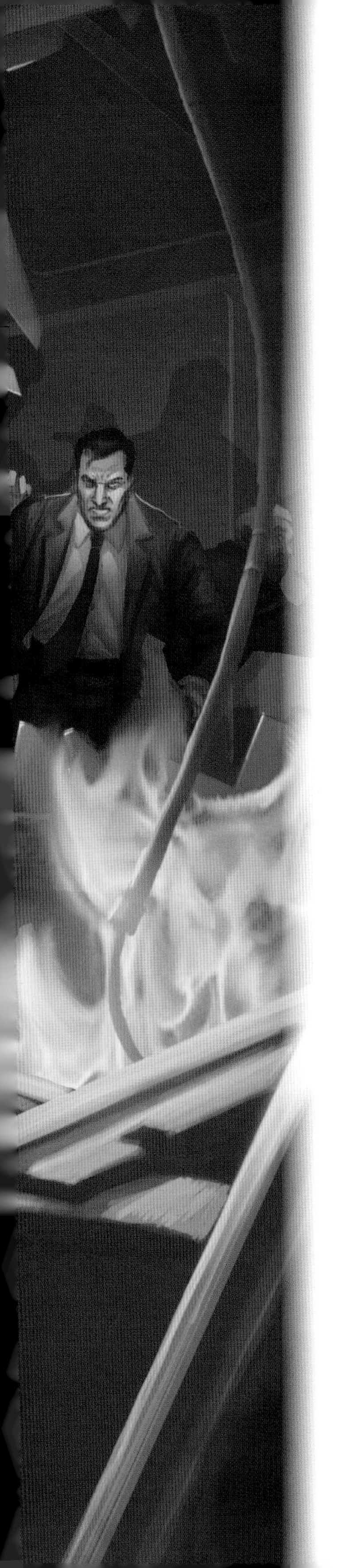

But Steve, in his new Super-Soldier body, was safe. The army put Steve through a very special training camp to teach him how to use his new body.

The general presented Steve with a special shield made of the strongest metal known and a unique costume to help Steve mask his identity.

With the costume and shield, Steve would now be known as America's most powerful soldier ...

CAPTAIN AMERICA!

In order to keep his secret safe, the general asked Steve to pretend to be a clumsy army private.

But when no one was looking, Steve donned his costume and fought for justice.

No one ever suspected that the worst private in the US Army was also the best soldier that the army had.

Captain America kept on fighting for liberty, until finally ... THE WAR HAD BEEN WON.

Though the country might not always live up to its promises, as long as Steve was able, he vowed to protect it and its ideals: justice, equality, freedom …

… and the dream of what the nation he loved could accomplish.

# THOR

## ORIGIN STORY

This is a story about someone who was born into royalty but needed to earn his honour.

This is a story about

a hero named THOR.

Thor's realm was called Asgard.

It sat like an island – its shores were swept by the sea of space. The people who lived on Asgard were called Asgardians and the Asgardians called our world Midgard. The only way to reach our world from theirs was by the rainbow bridge, Bifrost.

The bridge was guarded by a sentry called Heimdall. Even though Asgard was well-protected, threats were endless. Thor was one of the land's great protectors.

He was also a prince. He lived with his brother, Loki, in the castle of their father, Odin.

Thor was arrogant and chose his friends for their loyalty: the brave warrior Balder and a band of soldiers called the Warriors Three – Fandral, Volstagg and Hogun – and the beautiful, strong and wise Lady Sif.

Thor's father, Odin,
ruled over all of Asgard.

He and his wife, Frigga,
wanted nothing more than
for their sons to grow up
to be worthy rulers.

But there could only be one supreme ruler of Asgard. Only one who could be like Odin. And even though Loki was thoughtful, clever and quick, Thor was firstborn and so the throne was his by right.

To determine when Thor would be ready to rule, Odin had a special hammer made. It was forged from a mystical metal called Uru, which came from the heart of a dying star.

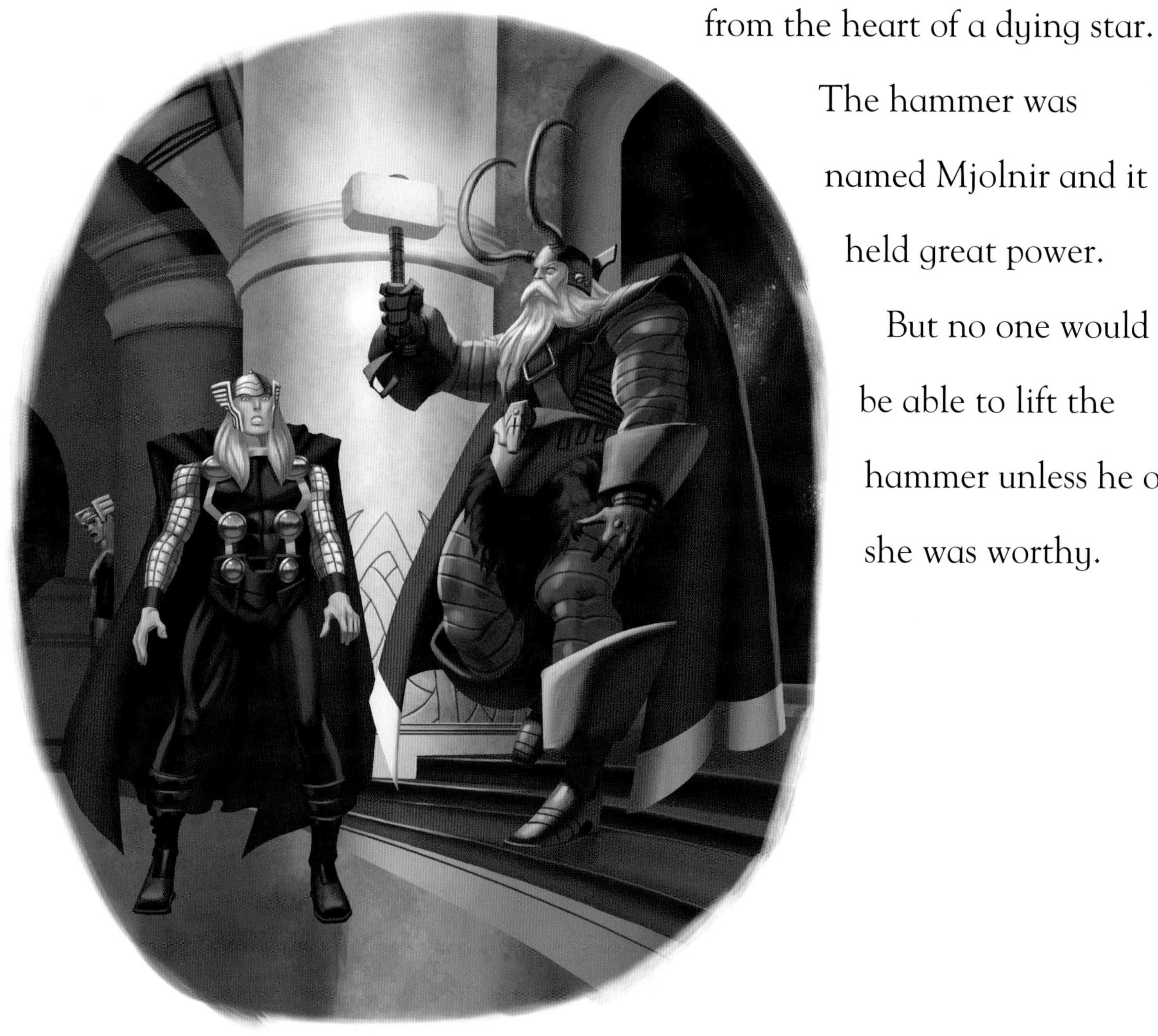

The hammer was named Mjolnir and it held great power.

But no one would be able to lift the hammer unless he or she was worthy.

The hammer was immovable to Thor.

Still, Odin's actions made it clear: the hammer was meant for his firstborn son and no one else.

Even so, proving worthy of Mjolnir was not an easy task. Thor spent nearly every moment trying to earn his right to hold the hammer.

He performed amazing acts of bravery ...

… he was honoured for acts of nobility and he demonstrated feats of great strength and honour.

With every great achievement, Thor attempted once more to pick up Mjolnir. It seemed as if he would never raise the hammer more than a few inches from the ground.

And then one day ... he did.

Thor had proved himself worthy of his weapon and he used it well.

When he threw the hammer, it always returned to him.

When he twirled it by its handle, he could soar like a winged beast!

And when he stamped it twice upon the ground ...

... he could summon all the powers of lightning, rain and thunder! In fact, with his hammer in hand, there was little Thor could not do.

And he knew it. Odin wanted him to be a great warrior and he had become one. His father wanted him to earn the respect of Asgard.

He had it. But then Thor began to let the power go to his head. And Odin was not happy. In fact, he had grown quite angry with his son.

Odin called Thor to his throne room. Thor knew that something was wrong. His father rarely summoned him in such a harsh tone. Thor was sure that his jealous brother, Loki, had span some lie to get him into trouble.

But nothing could have been further from Thor's mind than what Odin had to say to him.

Odin told Thor that he was his favoured son. He told him that he was brave beyond compare and noble as a prince must be.

He told him that his strength was legendary and that he was the best warrior in the kingdom. But Thor did not know what it meant to be weak or to feel pain. And without knowing humility, Thor could never be a truly honourable warrior.

Odin was angry. In his rage, he tore Mjolnir from Thor's hand and threw it towards Midgard. Then he stripped Thor of his armour and sent him to Earth.

Odin made his son believe that he was a medical student, with an injured leg, named Don Blake.

As Blake, Thor learned to study hard.

At times he thought he might fail. But he worked harder than he ever had in Asgard and in the end he earned his degree.

He allowed others to help him with his injury. In doing so, he discovered that people were generally good. Thor learned to truly love humanity. As a surgeon, he treated the sick.

He helped weak people find their strengths. And one day, while on holiday in Norway ...

... Don Blake found himself trapped in a cave.

The only possible exit lay behind a boulder.

He found a staff on the ground and shoved it under the boulder. He tried with all his might to move the rock. He pushed and pushed.

Nothing. He was so angry that he took the staff and struck it on the ground. And that's when it became clear that it was no ordinary stick.

It was Mjolnir in disguise! Odin had sent Don to this cave. Odin, the All Father of Asgard, was pleased.

His son had learned humility. He had, at long last, become a complete hero. He had become human in spirit, but still,

now

and forever,

he was ...

THE MIGHTY THOR.

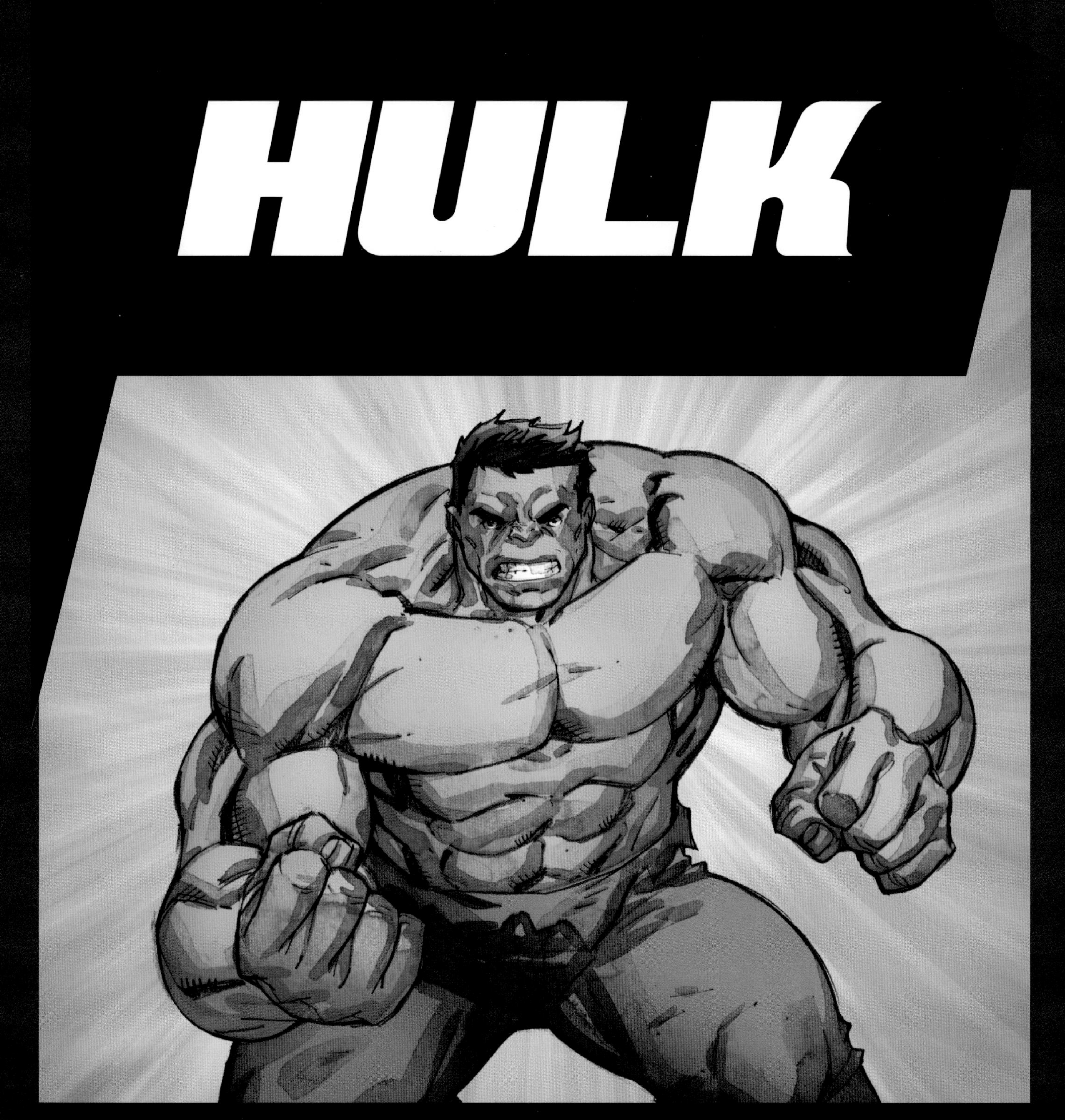


# ORIGIN STORY

**BRUCE BANNER** was not always **STRONG.**

He was not always **POWERFUL.**

And he was not always able to do **INCREDIBLE** things.

But most of all, Bruce was not always feared.

In fact, when he was young,

Bruce was mostly **AFRAID.**

He was often sad and nervous, and he didn't have a lot of friends.

But he was always ready to **HELP** someone in need.

Bruce kept all his feelings buried deep inside him.

Reading books about **SCIENCE** always took his mind off things.

And so, Bruce spent an awful lot of time with those books.

As Bruce grew older he continued to read, study, and learn.

... but he never learned how to talk about his **FEELINGS.**

Bruce became a doctor of science who worked for the army. He worked very hard both day and night. He was studying a type of energy called **GAMMA RADIATION.**

It was very dangerous, so he needed to be careful when he was near it. He wanted to find a way to use its power for **GOOD.**

Bruce decided the best way to test the gamma rays' power was to cause a massive explosion.

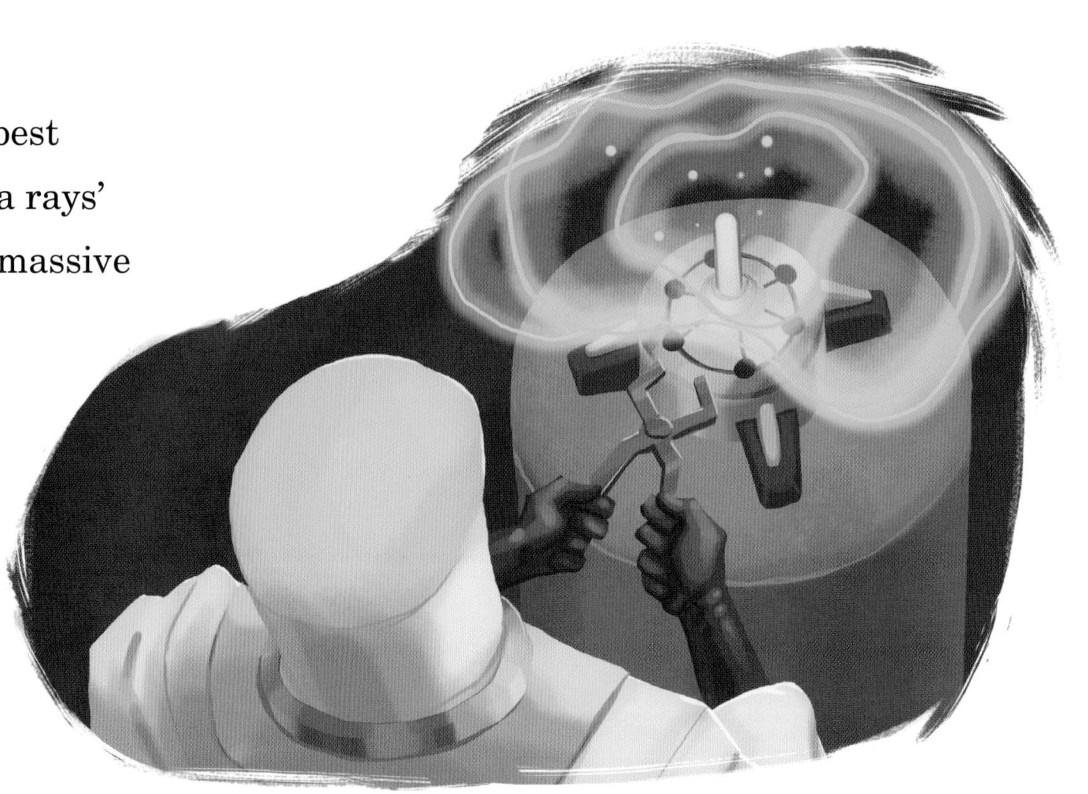

He would then measure the dangerous gamma radiation with special equipment.

## GENERAL 'THUNDERBOLT' ROSS

was in charge of the army lab where Bruce worked. He was angry with Bruce. The general had been waiting far too long to find out how much power the gamma rays held.

He needed to know.

**RIGHT NOW!**

But Bruce needed time to make sure the device was safe. He did not want anyone to get hurt. This made General Ross even angrier, and he yelled at Bruce some more.

Deep inside, Bruce remembered how upset he felt when people yelled at him as a child.

So he listened to the general's orders and sent the device to a safe area in the desert to be tested.

Soon, the countdown began. But just then, Bruce noticed something on his computer screen. He looked through his telescope to see what was wrong.

Someone had driven right into the danger zone! Bruce rushed out of the lab.

He couldn't let anyone be hurt by his experiment. Bruce told the teenager in the car that he needed to leave the site **RIGHT AWAY.**

But Bruce quickly realized they did not have time to clear the area!

He pushed the boy to safety inside a nearby shelter.

5 . . . 4 . . . 3 . . .
2 . . . 1 . . .

SAFE

Bruce woke up in an army hospital.

The teenager was there, too. Bruce learned the boy's name was **RICK JONES.** Rick thanked Bruce for saving his life.

Bruce was happy that Rick was safe.

He was also happy to be alive.

But then he looked around. He was locked up.

He remembered the blast.

He felt so scared, so confused and so helpless. Just the way he had when he was young.

Bruce felt **TRAPPED.**

And then something **CHANGED** in Bruce.

The soldiers didn't know that the gamma rays had transformed Bruce! They didn't recognize Bruce. They called him a ...

The army tried to stop the Hulk. But the Hulk just wanted to leave.

He didn't want to hurt anyone. He only wanted to be left alone.

So when he noticed that his actions put the soldiers in harm's way ...

Hulk knew he needed to help.

**"HULK SMASH!"**

he cried.

The Hulk had saved the soldiers and leaped away before he did any more damage.

And not long after he transformed back into **BRUCE BANNER.** Bruce didn't know if he would ever change into the Hulk again. He thought it best to hide out and lay low.

All the time, he wondered just how he had become both a mere man and

**THE INCREDIBLE HULK.**

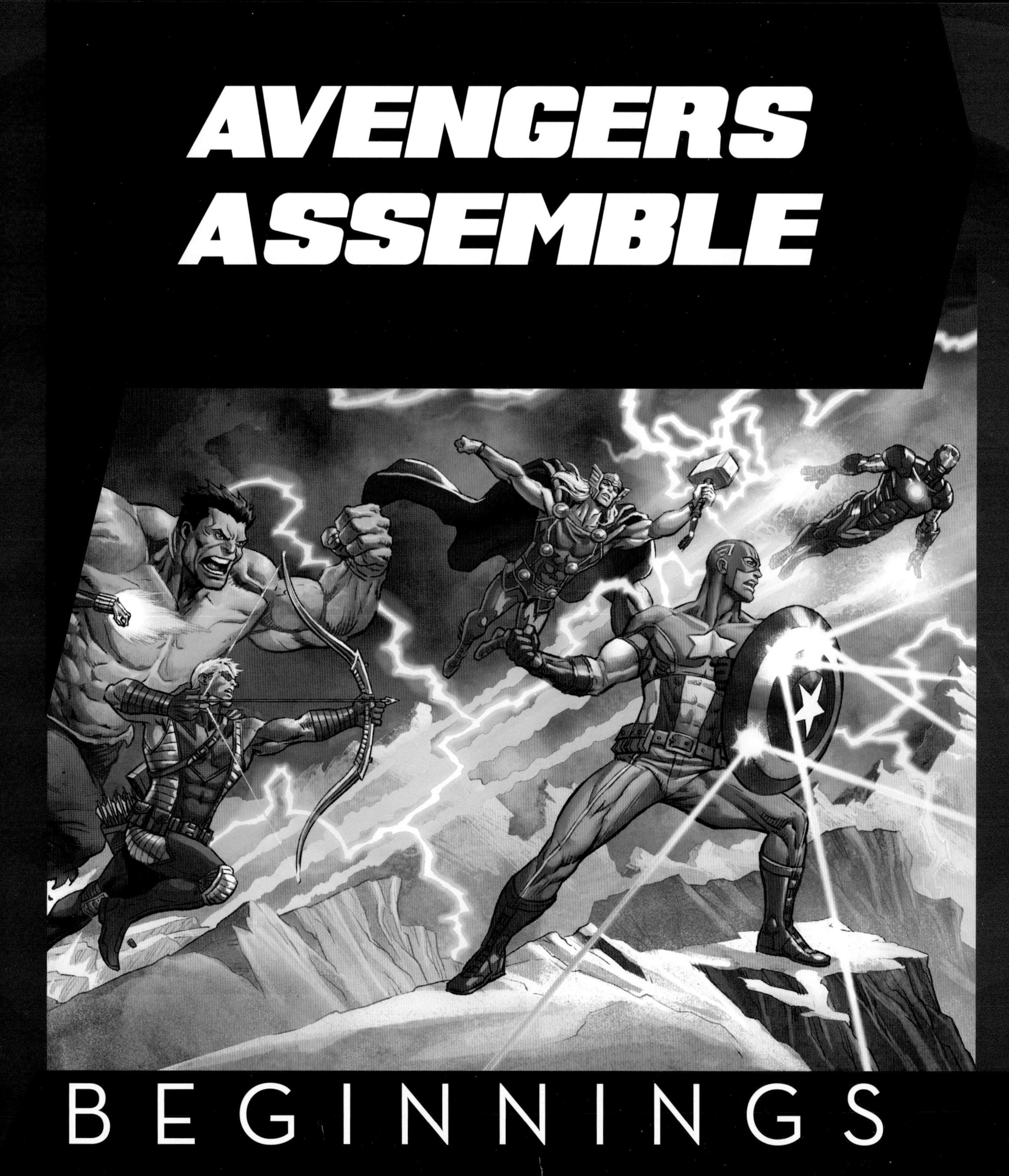
AVENGERS
ASSEMBLE
BEGINNINGS

A world filled with ideas, hope and potential will always attract a great many villains.

But for every villain that attacks,
there is a hero to defeat them....

Iron Man is known to the world as billionaire genius, Tony Stark. Tony built the suit for himself. The arc reactor technology within his chest keeps Tony's injured heart beating and powers the suit. People say the armour makes him powerful ...

Some might even say invincible.

Tony is not the only Super Hero.

Natasha Romanoff spent years training to be a top secret spy, handling missions some thought to be myth.

Eventually, Natasha was recruited by Nick Fury and S.H.I.E.L.D., where she was given high-tech equipment and the code name 'Black Widow'.

And Black Widow can always rely on Hawkeye.

Orphaned at an early age, Clint Barton worked for a travelling circus as a master archer. After witnessing Iron Man rescue people in danger, Clint knew that he too wanted to be a Super Hero and help those in need.

Clint made a costume and all manner of trick arrows, equipped with exploding tips, stunners and electrical nets. He became known as Hawkeye and joined the mighty Avengers.

And when Hawkeye's arrows aren't enough, there is always ... the Hulk!

After being exposed to gamma radiation, scientist Bruce Banner spent most of his life on the run. He always tried to stay calm because sometimes his emotions could get the better of him ...

Banner can transform into a huge green hero, who's always ready to save the day. But no matter how much he tries to help, people find it very hard to trust him. So the Hulk mostly keeps to himself.

Far away, in a place called Asgard, Thor made someone very angry. His brother, Loki, wanted to rule Asgard – or anywhere else for that matter. So Thor imprisoned his brother on a place called the Isle of Silence.

Loki didn't take this well. He wanted revenge!

Loki used his powers to search the Earth – a place his brother loves and has sworn to protect – to find someone people feared. Someone they distrusted. But, above all, someone who could defeat his brother, Thor.

Loki soon found someone – the Incredible Hulk!

The master of mischief, Loki, used his powers to trick the Hulk into thinking a high-speed train was about to crash on a broken train track.

The Hulk stopped the train, thinking he had saved the day.

But the broken track was just an illusion. The people on the train thought the Hulk was trying to hurt them. Word spread fast – the Hulk was on a rampage!

Soon after, the most powerful heroes in the world arrived to save the day.

But Loki had only wanted to lure Thor there, not the others! The Hulk might have been able to crush Thor, but he wouldn't stand a chance against four Super Heroes.

Loki used his powers again to create a version of the Hulk that only Thor could see. Then Loki returned to Asgard, and Thor chased after the fake Hulk!

But when Thor tried to strike the Hulk, his mighty hammer went right through him.

“An illusion!” Thor said – and he knew it could only be the work of Loki. Thor rushed back to Asgard and confronted his brother. Like the true coward he was … Loki ran.

But Thor grabbed Loki and brought him down to Earth once again.

Thor found the other heroes. They had cornered the real Hulk, who still thought he had done something wrong. Thor dropped Loki into the middle of the battle.

"Thou must know – this is your true villain! My brother, Loki of Asgard, tricked you into believing our comrade, the Hulk, smashed the train!"

And with that, Loki used his magic against the heroes. He created multiple illusions of himself. The Avengers didn't know which was the real Loki, so they attacked them all.

But one hero would not be tricked.

The group liked working together. They realized that as individuals, they were just Super Heroes. But as a team, they were a mighty, unstoppable force! So they became ...

# the Avengers!

So whenever big threats arose, the Avengers assembled once more. Because there will always be villains in the world....

After completing a mission in the Arctic Circle, where they had battled Namor, the Prince of Atlantis, the Avengers rode off in their submarine.

But soon, they spotted something floating in the distance. It looked like something frozen in a block of ice!

The Incredible Hulk swam to the figure and took it back to the sub. He took the block to the medical bay. There was a man trapped inside!

Iron Man slowly thawed the ice, to reveal ...

... Captain America! The famous super-soldier from World War II!

Cap had saved the world from the evil organisation HYDRA and its leader, Red Skull. But he was trapped in ice and had been there for decades!

Confused and on guard, Cap listened to the Avengers explain what had happened. They told him they were friends.

But before the group could get too friendly, the sub suddenly shook.

Namor was back and he'd brought an army of Atlanteans with him!

The Avengers fought hard, but they were no match for an entire army. They were overwhelmed.

But then someone who was not an Avenger stepped in ...

... and the tide began to turn! The Avengers, together with Captain America, defeated Namor and his army. They had stopped him from waging war on the surface world.

They were proud of the way they had worked together. The final member of their team was in place. Captain America raised his shield and the others rallied around him.

A new team had been born: Thor, Hulk, Hawkeye, Black Widow, Iron Man ... and now, Captain America!

The world would soon realize this group was something mighty.

And if a threat were ever to arise that was too big for one hero ... the Avengers would assemble!

# GUARDIANS OF THE GALAXY

## BEGINNINGS

The Universe is vast and beautiful, and within it live both good and evil. And sometimes, evil goes looking for a fight.

That's when a group of heroes comes forth to save the day. These heroes are ... the

# Guardians of the Galaxy!

Led by Star-Lord, the Guardians of the Galaxy vow to protect those in need.
But Star-Lord hasn't always been a hero. His story started on that tiny planet behind him, when he was just a little boy named Peter Quill.

Like all children, Peter played outside and read comic books, and he was fascinated by the stars and the galaxy. He also believed in doing the right thing. Peter stood up for himself and protected others. Even then Peter was a Guardian.

And when Peter grew up, he became a Guardian of the Earth as ...

## ... Star-Lord!

After years of travelling across the galaxy as a carefree space explorer, Peter realized he needed a change. He missed his friends and family – and he knew of the evil in the Universe, ready to wipe out his loved ones when it got the chance.

Peter needed to protect his home planet, but he couldn't do it alone.

First, he met Gamora.

With her people enslaved and her village destroyed by the Badoon – a warlike empire intent on destroying all things good, including Earth – young Gamora fled her planet. She was very young and very scared.

Taken in by Thanos, the most feared villain in the Universe, Gamora was raised to be a dangerous warrior.

But after many years, Gamora realized Thanos was just like the Badoon, so she fled once again, vowing always to fight evil.

Gamora agreed to join Star-Lord.

Star-Lord and Gamora met a great warrior named Drax the Destroyer!

Legend had it that Drax had become so enraged when he lost his family to the Badoon, that he defeated one of their fighter ships all by himself!

Since then, Drax had travelled the galaxy, fighting for good, living by his own moral code and desiring peace for everyone.

Knowing what it was like to lose a family, as both Star-Lord and Gamora had, Drax agreed to join their team.

Far away, in another part of the Universe, there was Planet X: a beautiful world filled with sprawling forests and tree-like beings who had the ability to grow larger, or regrow from a single leaf. They studied humans and their environment.

One being in particular wanted to know more about the human race. His name was Groot. Although his speech was limited, it was clear when Star-Lord met Groot that he had decided to join the quest.

The final member of the team was the one called Rocket Raccoon.

But he was no ordinary raccoon. He was born a fierce fighter on the planet known as Halfworld. Scientists noticed Rocket and gave him advanced skills. He learned to use his new talents to do what he loved most: making new weapons! And firing them at bad guys was his speciality!

So Rocket also joined Star-Lord and his team.

Word of this new alliance travelled fast in space, and it didn't take long for the Badoon to learn of Peter's plan to protect Earth.

So the team of misfits and outlaws quickly suited up ...

... and the Guardians of the Galaxy were born!

Rocket was the brains of the operation. He helped the Guardians out of seemingly hopeless situations.

Groot's ability to change in size and regrow when injured made him a trusted ally. But he also had heart, which could be useful, too.

Drax's strength – and reputation as the Destroyer – made him a force to be reckoned with.

Gamora's warrior training, combined with her vast knowledge of the galaxy, was invaluable to the Guardians.

Star-Lord had found his team to help him protect Earth. They trusted him and followed his lead across the galaxy.

The Badoon were ready to conquer Earth at all costs.

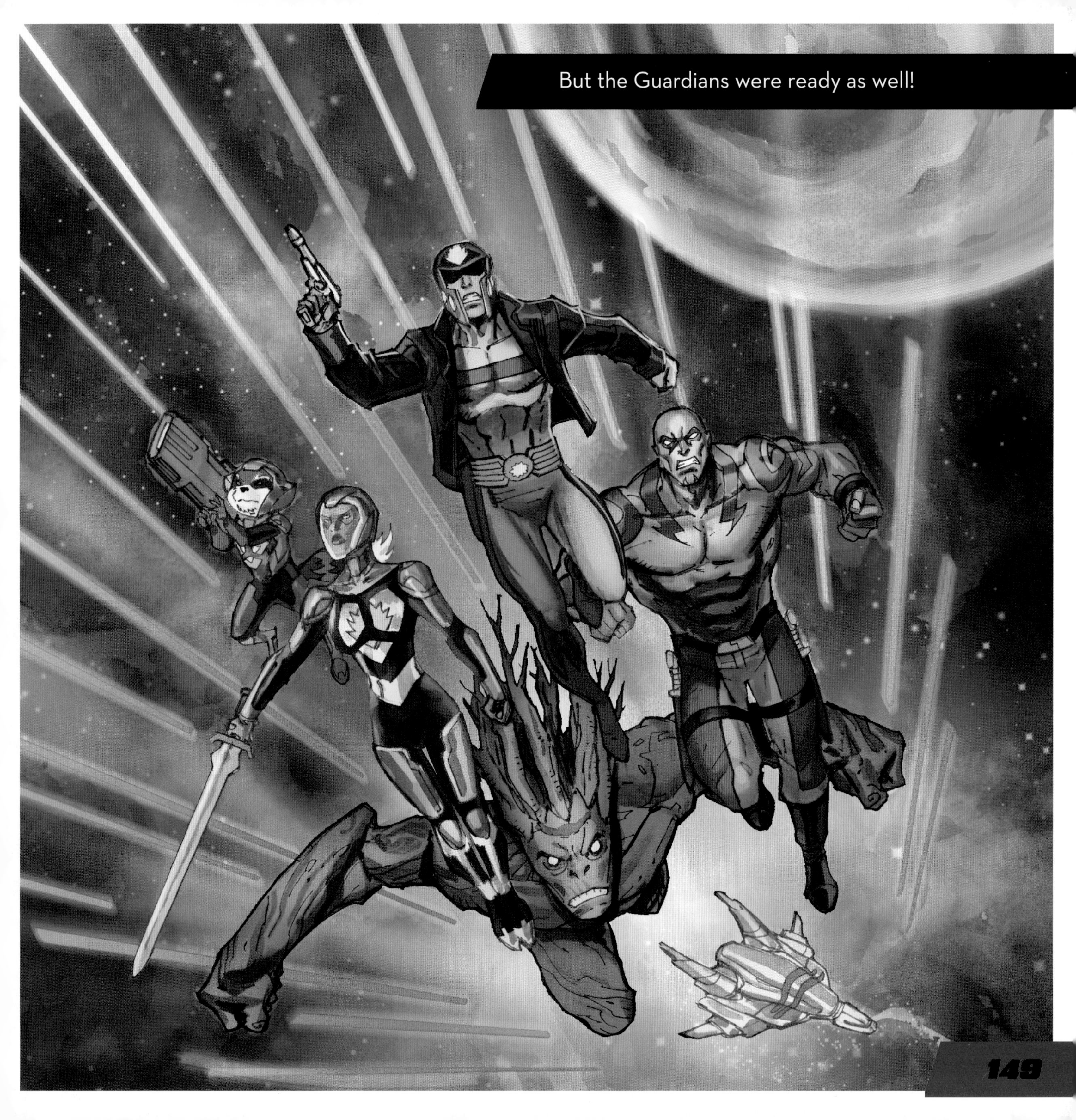
But the Guardians were ready as well!

The Guardians fought with heart, battling long and hard.

Gamora, Drax and Star-Lord worked as a team and tore through the Badoon with ease. Groot grew and grew, towering over the Badoon, while Rocket used his arsenal of weapons to blast at the invading aliens.

And when one needed help, another stepped up to lend a hand!

The battle raged on, until finally ...

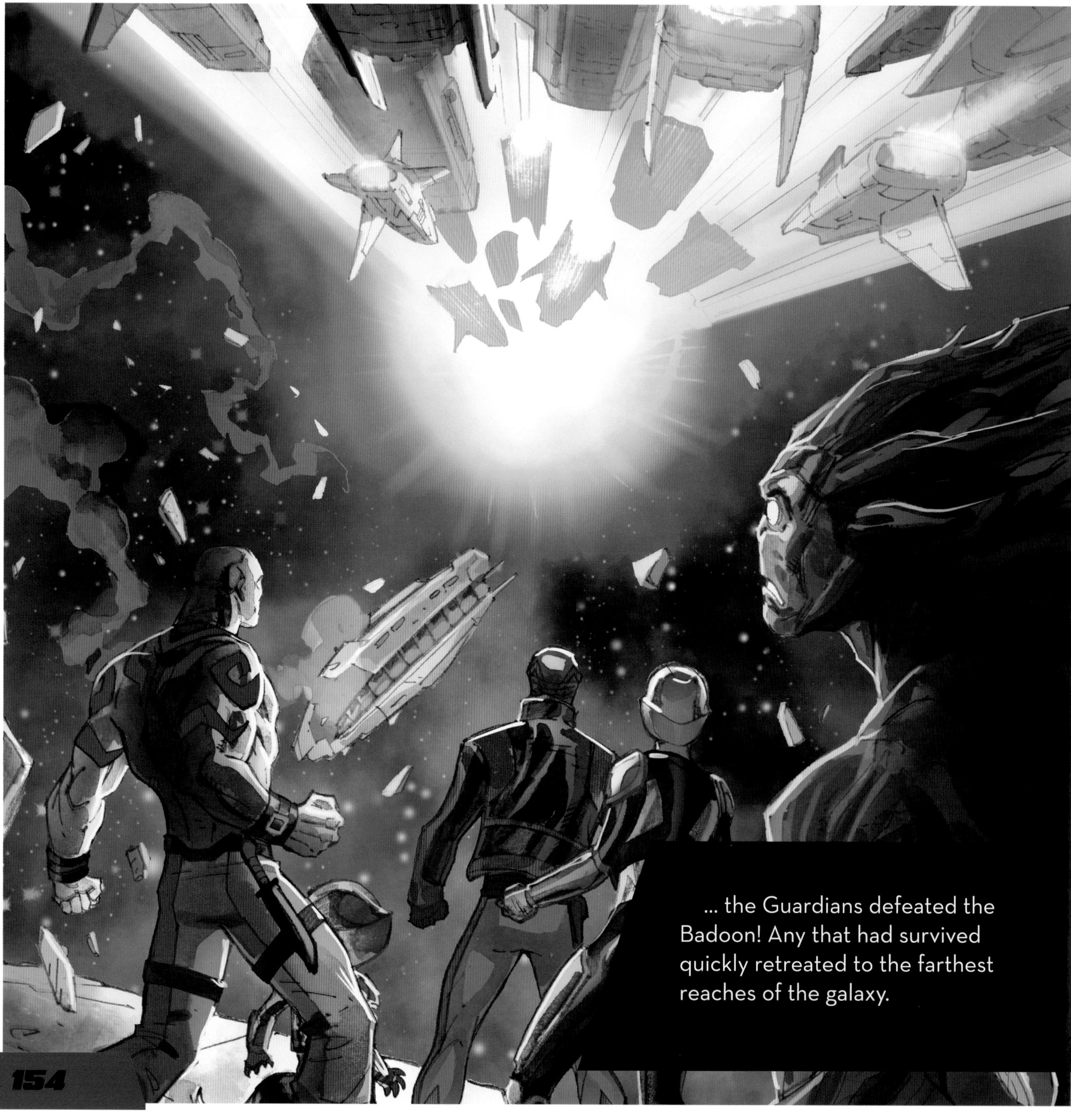

... the Guardians defeated the Badoon! Any that had survived quickly retreated to the farthest reaches of the galaxy.

Peter knew stopping the Badoon was a symbol of hope – for the galaxy, for Earth, for his friends and family.

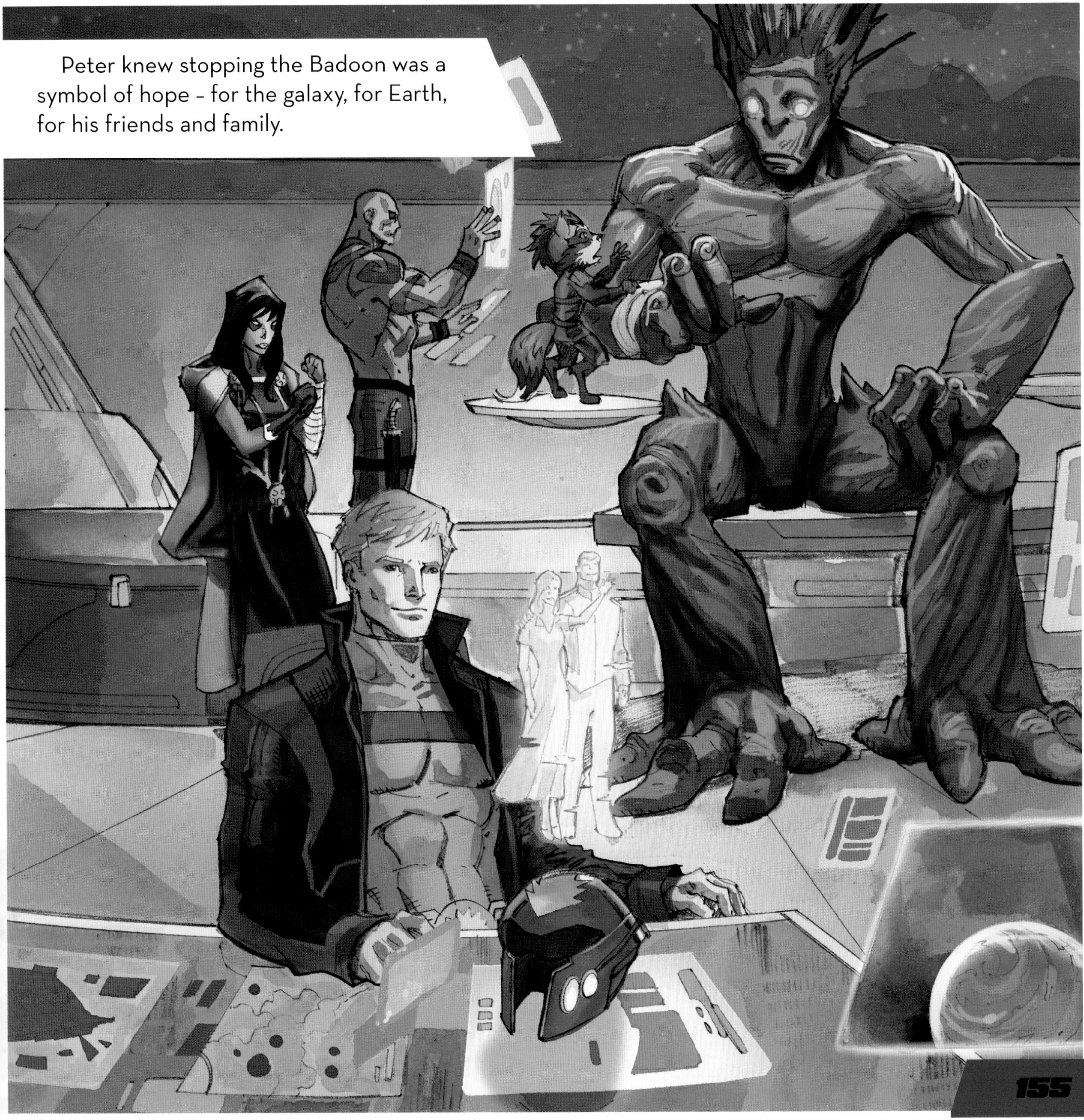

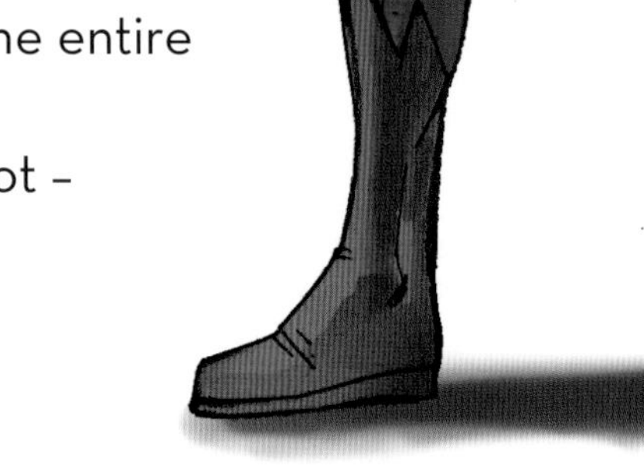

Peter dreamed that, one day, the entire galaxy would be free from evil.

Gamora, Drax, Rocket and Groot – they too shared Peter's dream.

And from that day forward, those who fought against peace would answer to ... the Guardians of the Galaxy!